Tyrese and the Three Dogs Plus a Cat

Created by
Eric Marcus Jean-Baptiste
and Eddy Jean-Baptiste Junior

Written By

Ketly Pierre
Author of "Poems from the Heart"

To order additional copies of this book, contact:
Xlibris
844-714-8691
www.Xlibris.com
Orders@Xlibris.com

ISBN: 978-1-4257-8694-6 (sc)
ISBN: 978-1-4363-1342-1 (hc)

Print information available on the last page

Rev. date: 05/30/2025

Tyrese and the Three Dogs Plus a Cat

Illustrated By

Ketly Pierre

Dedication

From Ketly- Thanks to my God, Eric, Eddy for helping me to write this book and to my families and friends who have supported me. I love you mommy, Ruth Juste, for being you.

Thank you, God, for blessing me with my grandmothers Ruth Juste and Anne Jean-Baptiste for loving me. To my parents Nehemi and Eddy Jean-Baptiste Sr. for believing in us, that we can do anything and the sky is the limit to reach all our dreams and love to all my families and friends.

A special thanks to God for blessing us with Auntie Keket "Ketly P. Mondesir" to be our guide and light to create our first book together. We love you always.

This story begins with a little boy named Tyrese who had three dogs. The first dog's name was Dubuisson, the second dog's name was Eddy and the third dog's name was Marcus. Plus a cat named Meme. They all lived in a farm filled with lots of animals and laughter. Until one day a wolf named Fred tried to steal the chickens and the eggs from the barn.

7

One day, Dubuisson was taking a walk near the farm. He saw the wolf, named Fred. The wolf was trying to steal the chickens and the eggs from the barn. Dubuisson barked to make the wolf run away. Then, Tyrese and the other animals heard him barking. The animals included Tyrese walked toward the barn to join Dubuisson."The wolf Fred was trying to steal the chickens and the eggs from the barn," said Dubuisson. So, they decided to make a trap for the wolf.

The first trap they decided to make was fake eggs. Tyrese, the dogs, and the cat looked for rocks that were shaped like an egg and painted it white. Marcus removed the real eggs and placed the fake eggs in that same spot. Tyrese and the others decided to pretend to be sleeping; so they could catch the wolf. However, they were so tired of waiting on Fred the wolf they all fell asleep.

Fred, the wolf noticed the animals and Tyrese were sleeping. Fred, the wolf, entered quietly inside the barn. He walked towards the chickens and eggs. Then, he picked up one of egg up. Fred, the wolf, felt the egg was too heavy to be a real egg. Smart as he is. Fred, the wolf, put it back down. Instead, he grabbed a chicken and ran out of the barn. Tyrese and the others woke up the next day and decided to go inside the barn to see if the wolf had taken the fake eggs. They noticed the fake eggs were still there. However, a chicken was missing. That made them angry. So, they decided to make a second plan that would protect the eggs and the chickens better.

The second trap they decided to make was to dig a big hole so the wolf can fall inside of it. Tyrese, the dogs, and the cat dug a big hole and covered it with fake grass. They surrounded the area with fake chickens and eggs. This time Tyrese decided he would stay up to catch the wolf called Fred while the others were sleeping. However, Tyrese was so tired he fell asleep again.

Fred, the wolf, came when he knew they would be sleeping. He entered quietly inside the barn. He noticed there were no chickens or eggs there, but it was on the other side of the barn. He decided to walk to the other side of the barn when he realized the chicken did not move as he got closer. Smart as he was, Fred the wolf turned around and saw the real chickens in the coop as he grabbed another chicken and ran out of the barn.

The next day, Tyrese, the three dogs, and the cat walked to the other side of the barn. To see if the wolf named Fred has fallen inside the hole. However, they noticed the fake chickens and eggs are still in the same spot. Eddy decided to walk toward the coop to see if real chickens are still there and he noticed one was missing again. So they decided to make a third plan.

The third trap they decided to make were chickens to move with a remote. Tyrese and the dogs made chips and put it inside the fake chickens. So it could move with the remote control. The cat made the fake eggs look and feel real. This time, Eddy decided he would be the one to stay up to make the chicken move. "Remember Fred, the wolf, is very smart. He comes when we are sleeping," said Meme the cat. Tyrese decided he was smarter than Fred, the wolf by telling the others to pretend to be sleeping, so the wolf would come.

Tyrese, the dogs, and the cat pretended to be sleeping. The wolf crawled slowly from behind the tree and entered the barn. Tyrese and the others opened their eyes just enough to see what the wolf was doing as Marcus made the chickens move with the remote control. Fred, the wolf noticed the chickens were moving, so he grabbed the fake chicken and eggs ran out of the barn.

The moment the wolf ran out of the barn. Tyrese and the animals opened their eyes and laughed. Fred, the wolf, did not know the chickens and eggs were fake; and it's was controlled by the remote controller.

Eddy pressed the button on the remote control to blow the wolf to the moon. They never saw the wolf called Fred ever again.

The End

Printed in the United States
by Baker & Taylor Publisher Services